D1758445

A2 987 772 0

ISBN 978-0-86037-96-1

MUSLIM CHILDREN'S LIBRARY
General Editors: Khurram Murad and Mushuq Ally

THE PERSECUTOR COMES HOME
Author: Khurram Murad
Editing: Mardijah A. Tarantino
Illustrations: Bookmatrix
Cover Design: Nasir Cadir
Coordinator: Anwar Cara

These stories are about the Prophet and his Companions and, though woven around authentic ahadith, should only be regarded as stories.

Published by

THE ISLAMIC FOUNDATION,
Markfield Conference Centre,
Ratby Lane, Markfield,
Leicestershire, LE67 9SY, United Kingdom
Website: www.islamic-foundation.org.uk

QURAN HOUSE, P.O. Box 30611, Nairobi, Kenya

P.M.B. 3193, Kano, Nigeria

All enquiries to:
Kube Publishing
Tel: +44(0)1530 249230, Fax +44(0)1530 249656
Email: info@kubepublishing.com
www.kubepublishing.com

A catalogue record of this book is available from British Library

The Persecutor Comes Home

Story of Umar

Khurram Murad

Oldham Libraries

MUSLIM CHILDREN'S LIBRARY

An Introduction

Here is a new series of books, but with a difference, for children of all ages. Published by the Islamic Foundation, the Muslim Children's Library has been produced to provide young people with something they cannot perhaps find anywhere else.

Most of today's children's books aim only to entertain and inform or to teach some necessary skills, but not to develop the inner and moral resources. Entertainment and skills by themselves impart nothing of value to life unless a child is also helped to discover deeper meaning in himself and the world around him. Yet there is no place in them for God, who alone gives meaning to life and the universe, nor for the divine guidance brought by His prophets, following which can alone ensure an integrated development of the total personality.

Such books, in fact, rob young people of access to true knowledge. They give them no unchanging standards of right and wrong, nor any incentives to live by what is right and refrain from what is wrong. The result is that all too often the young enter adult life in a state of social alienation and bewilderment, unable to cope with the seemingly unlimited choices of the world around them. The situation is especially devastating for the Muslim child as he may grow up cut off from his culture and values.

The Muslim Children's Library aspires to remedy this deficiency by showing children the deeper meaning of life and the world around them by pointing them along paths leading to an integrated development of all aspects of their personality; by helping to give them the capacity to cope with the complexities of their world, both personal and social; by opening vistas into a world extending far beyond this life; and, to a Muslim child especially, by providing a fresh and strong faith, a dynamic commitment, an indelible sense of identity, a throbbing yearning and an urge to struggle, all rooted in !slam.

The books aim to help a child anchor his development on the rock of divine guidance, and to understand himself and relate to himself and others in just and meaningful ways. They relate directly to his soul and intellect, to his emotions and imagination, to his motives and desires, to his anxieties and hopes — indeed, to every aspect of his fragile, but potentially rich personality. At the same time it is recognised that for a book to hold a child's attention, he must enjoy reading it; it should therefore arouse his curiosity and entertain him as well. The style, the language, the illustrations and the production of the books are all geared to this goal. They provide moral education, but not through sermons or ethical abstractions.

Although these books are based entirely on Islamic teachings and the vast Muslim heritage, they should be of equal interest and value to all children, whatever their country or creed; for Islam is a universal religion, the natural path.

Adults, too, may find much of use in them. In particular, Muslim parents and teachers will find that they provide what they have for so long been so badly needing. The books will include texts on the Qur'an, the Sunnah and other basic sources and teachings of Islam, as well as history, stories and anecdotes for supplementary reading. Each book will cater for a particular age group, classified into five: pre-school, 5-8 years, 8-11, 11-14 and 14-17.

We invite parents and teachers to use these books in homes and classrooms, at breakfast tables and bedside and encourage children to derive maximum benefit from them. At the same time their greatly valued observations and suggestions are highly welcome.

To the young reader we say: you hold in your hands books which may be entirely different from those you have been reading till now, but we sincerely hope you will enjoy them; try, through these books, to understand youself, your life, your experiences and the universe around you. They will open before your eyes new paths and models in life that you will be curious to explore and find exciting and rewarding to follow.

May God be with you forever. And may He bless with His mercy and acceptance our humble contribution to the urgent and gigantic task of producing books for a new generation of people, a task which we have undertaken in all humility and hope.

Khurram Jah Murad
Director General

8

Umar could not sleep any longer. He got out of bed, opened the door of his house and went outside. The full moon shone above the rooftops and the streets were empty and still. After a while Umar noticed a man walking briskly towards the Ka'ba. His steps were measured, and he walked as if he was climbing a gentle slope. He was neither tall nor short, yet he seemed to tower over all his surroundings. Umar immediately recognised him as being the man he hated most. The man who had brought so much trouble to the people of Makka by calling them

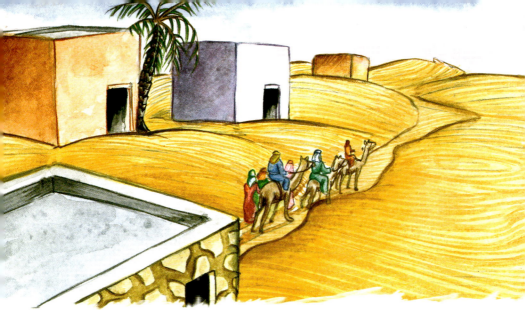

to a new religion. The man who challenged all the gods
they had been worshipping for ages as false and powerless
and, instead, invited them to serve the One God alone.
The man who had divided the Quraysh, father against son,
brother against brother, husband against wife.

As Umar watched Muhammad (Peace and Blessings be
upon him)*, for that is who it was walking towards the
Ka'ba, he was reminded of the very scene which had kept
him restless all night, causing him to wander out into the
street, while everyone else was sleeping.

Umm Abdullah's lovely face flashed before his eyes. 'Yes,
Umar, you have made life unbearable for us', she had
told him. His own cousin, Umm Abdullah, (a member
of one of the most respected families of Makka), had
defied him and was leaving for Abyssinia with many other
young men and women who were following Muhammad.
Umar had never imagined that Umm Abdullah would

* Muslims are required to invoke Allah's blessings and peace upon the
Prophet whenever his name is mentioned.

be amongst those who would be forced to leave Makka. True, he had been responsible for making life miserable for Muhammad's companions. As a result, one by one they had deserted their families, and each broken family filled Umar with greater wrath against Muhammad. Yet he never thought that they would leave even their ancestral homes.

That morning he had gone to Umm Abdullah's house to see what her plans were, and had found her in the midst of making preparations for a long journey. Umar had said: 'What, you too are leaving?' and she had replied with those words, so full of hurt and reproach. 'Yes, Umar, you have made life unbearable for us. Our only crime has been to believe in the One God. We have complete trust in Him. We know that He will guide and protect us so that we may be allowed to serve Him and worship Him in peace.'

On any other occasion, Umar would have hit her. The very thought was unbearable for him: members of his own tribe embracing Islam and following Muhammad, the renegade. But at the same time, the sight of these noble sons and daughters of the Quraysh leaving Makka for no other crime than that of professing a new faith,

filled him with grief. He had not been able to answer her. His heart ached and his eyes filled with tears. His mouth opened to utter a curse, but to his astonishment he found himself saying 'God be with you, then.'

Umm Abdullah was taken aback. She had never known Umar to be soft hearted. On the contrary, he was one of the fiercest, toughest men in Makka. A ray of hope entered her heart. Could it be that even the indomitable Umar would bend before the power of Truth?

In the evening, when her husband returned home, she told him about Umar's visit. She voiced her hope that Umar would some day at least be sympathetic to their cause, if not to embrace it.

'So, because he did not curse you, you think he might some day join us?', her husband 'Amir asked.

'Well, yes... I have some hope' she replied.

But 'Amir shook his head. 'Old Khattab's ass might embrace Islam, maybe, but Khattab's son? Hah! Never!'

Umar's conversation with Umm Abdullah had left a strong impression on him. His conscience was disturbed and he was ill at ease. Why should people who had lived all their lives in Makka be forced to leave only because their beliefs were different? Umar could not fully justify to himself the persecution which he in part had been responsible for. He hated himself for it, but because his pride would not allow him to admit it, he was condemned to sleepless nights.

It was on one of those nights that he saw the Blessed ` Prophet Muhammad on his way to the Ka'ba. The very sight of the man enraged him; was *he* not the root of all the trouble, the reason why families were split apart and young people were misled? And there he was... free to walk the streets and to worship in the Sacred House! Umar was furious. He muttered: 'Umar, you are the most feared man in Makka. You hate Islam and all that it stands for and, more than anything, you hate that wretched man *there* that strolls by your door as if he had none to fear! Therefore, you should keep an eye on him!'

And so saying, Umar followed the lonely silhouette down the streets to the Ka'ba. As he entered the Haram* the Blessed Prophet Muhammad was already there, facing north towards Jerusalem, performing his Prayers and glorifying God. Umar had never actually heard what Muhammad said he had received from God; because of prejudice and indifference, he did not want to hear.

* The sacred enclosure inside which stood the House of God, the Ka'ba, the Masjid al-Haram.

But Umm Abdullah's face appeared again before him as he stood in the darkness of the Haram, and his curiosity became aroused. What spell or magic could there *be* in those words to cause people to give up their livelihood and their customs to follow him? By God, Umar feared no man, no magic of any kind, for he was the strongest man in Makka!

Lifting his arm, he pushed aside the heavy cloth that draped the Ka'ba and hid behind it. Then he slowly

inched forward, nearer to the Blessed Prophet
Muhammad. 'Talk, Muhammad!' he muttered between
clenched teeth. 'Let us hear the magic words. Spin
your witchcraft for Umar!' As if in answer, the Blessed
Prophet Muhammad's voice rang out clearly:

'The Sure Reality!

What is the Sure Reality?

And what will make
Thee realise what
The Sure Reality is?'

Umar leaned forward so as not to miss a word.

'...And Pharaoh,
And those before him,
And the cities overthrown,
Committed habitual sin,

And disobeyed, each,
The Messenger of their Lord;
So he seized them
With an increasing penalty.

. . .

That day shall ye be
Brought to Judgement:
Not an act of yours
That ye hide will be hidden.

. . .

Then he that will be
Given his record
In his right hand
Will say: Ah here!
Read ye my record!

. . .

And he that will
Be given his record
In his left hand
Will say: Ah! would
That my record had not
Been given to me!

. . .

Of no profit to me
Has been my wealth!

My power has
Gone from me!

. . .

This was he that
Would not believe
In God Most High,
And would not urge
The feeding of the needy!

So no friend hath he
Here this Day.

Nor hath he any food
Except the foul pus
From the wounds...'

The fearful and penetrating words of the Qur'an struck
Umar to the heart. He caught his breath as if stunned, and
was forced to consider its meaning. 'Truly, it has power,
for I can recognise power... but it is in the form of poetry
...powerful poetry... that is it!

It is this poetry which has corrupted the people of the
Quraysh!'

But the Blessed Prophet Muhammad's words broke
through Umar's thoughts:

'...this is verily the word
Of an honoured Messenger.

It is not the word
Of a poet:
Little it is
Ye believe!'

Umar was completely taken aback. Was this man able to
read his thoughts? If he could read people's thoughts then
he must be a *Kahin*, a soothsayer, able to read the secrets
that lie in people's hearts! Again the Blessed Prophet
Muhammad's words held his attention:

'...Nor is it the word
Of a soothsayer:
Little it is
Ye remember

This is a Message
Sent down from the Lord
Of the Worlds.

And if the Messenger
Were to invent
Any sayings in Our name,

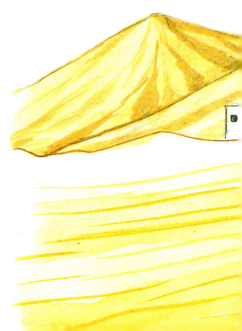

We should certainly seize him
By his right hand,

And We should certainly
Then cut off the artery
Of his heart...'

Never before had Umar been confronted with such a situation. The argument was overpowering. If Muhammad were lying, if he had *not* received a message from God, then surely his God would destroy him. Umar could take no more. Confused and perplexed, he stepped out from behind the curtain, turned his back on the Ka'ba, and walked slowly along the deserted road to his house.

Above the rooftops of Makka, a pink veil covered the sky, as if, in the receding darkness, a dawn of hope was rising over the city. So it was in Umar's turbulent heart. For a moment, it seemed as if the darkness had lifted, allowing a glimmer of understanding and faith to enter; but in fact, the real battle within Umar had just begun. He felt this glimmer of understanding to be a weakness, and this only increased his stubbornness and anger.

A part of him would have liked to wipe out all that he had heard that night, as well as the face and words of Umm Abdullah, so that he could remain undisturbed.

But this was not to be. Another part of him, deep within, recognised the Blessed Prophet Muhammad as being sincere; a man of integrity whose message was closer to the truth than anything Umar had ever learned from his forefathers... than all the superstition which had held his heart and mind in chains since his youth. Even so, he could not bring himself to give up the old beliefs for the sake of one man's claim. For the sake of a mere woman's words!

It was in this state of mind that Umar, under the pink light of dawn, entered his house and closed the door.

The newly converted Muslims were a tortured and persecuted minority in Makka. They could neither profess their faith openly nor could they pray in the Haram; and Umar's fierce opposition played a large part in creating this situation. They were few and their opponents and persecutors were many, but none of them was as active and zealous as Umar.

The Blessed Prophet's headquarters were located by the side of Mount Safa, in the house of his close companion, Arqam. His followers would come and stay with him for several days and nights at a time, learning the Quran by heart, talking with him about Islam, and discussing amongst themselves how best to survive in a community which had rejected them and how best to prepare themselves for the great struggle which they knew lay ahead.

The Blessed Prophet had divided his Muslim community into groups, and each group was entrusted to the care and guidance of one of the Blessed Prophet's senior followers. Besides coming to the house of Arqam, they would also visit each other's houses, reciting and remembering and understanding the latest revelations learnt from the Blessed Prophet, and recording on leaves and bits of

parchment the verses which were later to become the
Surahs of the Quran. Unbeknown to Umar, his own sister,
Fatimah, and her husband Sa'id, housed one of these
centres, for they had become Muslims.

One morning, in the Blessed Prophet's house, the
conversation had been particularly discouraging. News
had reached them that Abu Jahl, another fierce enemy of
Islam, and Umar had planned for several of the followers
to be beaten and insulted. It seemed to the group seated
in the Blessed Prophet's house that they had no other
recourse but to hide or flee. 'The trouble is, there aren't
enough of us to resist', said one. 'Look at us: some of us
former slaves, most of us too young! What can we do
against the mighty Quraysh? What we need is a few strong

people of our own!' The others smiled sadly in agreement, and they all sat thinking over what had just been said.

Slowly, the Blessed Prophet, who was sitting close by, raised his hands to God and prayed 'Oh Allah! Lend strength to Islam! Guide to Islam Abu Jahl, son of Hisham, or Umar, son of Khattab. Oh Allah! Whichever of these men you love more, guide him to Islam!' Everyone there who heard the prayer repeated it silently in his own heart, and when the Blessed Prophet sat down again, they murmured as if in one voice a quiet '*Amin*'.

Umar, meanwhile, was more miserable than ever. By night, the scene in the Haram continued to haunt him. The verses from the Quran which the Blessed Prophet had recited haunted his dreams and kept him from sleep: *That day shall ye be brought to judgement: not an act of yours that ye hide shall be hidden...* By day, Umar's fury against the Blessed Prophet grew and grew.

One particular morning, he reached a swift decision. 'Why, what is the matter with me?' he declared aloud, as he paced back and forth in his room. 'I see no problem at all! If there is a boil festering on your body, just slice it off! It's as simple as that!' He reached for his sword. 'If there is one scum destroying an entire city, then cut him down!' He was astonished that he had not thought of it before.

Umar, like all fierce men of action, believed that an idea could be crushed by force, and he could not wait once he had decided to use force. He had not yet understood that when a great truth, a great belief, is born amongst a people, and they are committed to it, it cannot be wiped out by force. Unaware of the forces that were surrounding him, Umar marched out of the house, sword in hand. To the passer-by in the street on that day in Makka, this rough giant wielding a naked sword would not easily go unnoticed.

It was not long before he came across his cousin Nu'aym, son of Abdullah al-Naham. Nu'aym's eyes fell upon the gleaming blade in Umar's fist. It did not speak well of his designs. Nu'aym tried to remain calm.

'Where to, Umar?' he asked.

Umar's face was white with determination. 'Where to? Hah! Good question. To put an end to it, that's what! Put an end to that heretic who has divided the Quraysh and condemns the religion of our forefathers! Who abuses our idols...'

Umar's voice rose to a high pitch and people living along the street peered fearfully from their windows at the sound.

'He shall condemn *no more*!' Umar's sword slashed the air.

Nu'aym's heart sank. How would he ever stop this fanatic?

Quickly he thought of something to say which would slow Umar's rush towards the Blessed Prophet's house. 'Whoever gave you the idea you could kill Muhammad and get away with it? Do you think that if you succeed, his family would leave you alive? Do you not realise what a blood retribution they would take on our tribe, the Banu Adi?'

Umar shouted back his answer and a terrible argument followed, each man out-yelling the other.

'I see now!' yelled Umar. 'You too are a heretic! Come here, and I shall cure you of your illness!'

Summoning up his courage, Nu'aym answered: 'You are so sure of yourself, Umar! You fool. You don't even know that your own sister is a Muslim. Yes, Fatimah! And her husband Sa'id. They're a lot wiser than you are. They don't stupidly cling to evil ways once they've heard the truth!'

'You lie!' gasped Umar, whose eyes bulged dangerously at this preposterous news.

Abruptly he shifted direction from the Blessed Prophet's house to that of his sister's. Nu'aym, seeing what he was about, tried to block the path, but Umar shoved him aside. 'Then they shall be the first to die!' he shouted, moving off with gigantic strides.

But the road leading to Fatimah's house was a long one, and by the time Umar reached her door some of his anger had spent itself. He stopped to catch his breath before pounding on the door with the butt of his sword, and in so doing he caught the sound of voices chanting in unison. He hesitated an instant, listening, then pounded on the door with all his strength.

Within, Fatimah, her husband Sa'id and Khabbab, the instructor, were reciting the most recent words of Allah they had been taught by the Blessed Prophet. They halted, shocked at the intrusion.

'Who is there?' called Fatimah.

'Umar, son of Khattab.'

At the sound of Umar's voice, Khabbab, a fragile man, disappeared into the inner room. 'Quick', whispered Sa'id, 'hide the parchments'. Fatimah slid them inside her garment, close to her chest, and quickly composed herself. Umar knocked again louder, and Sa'id opened the door, to reveal Umar's great form brandishing a sword. 'What was all that muttering? Don't think I didn't hear you!'

'Nothing', replied Fatimah calmly. 'We were just talking.'

'Liars! Cowards! I know you are heretics!'

Fatimah and Sa'id looked at each other. Now that Umar knew, there was nothing to conceal.

'The truth is not what you believe it to be', said Sa'id calmly.

This was too much for Umar. Losing all control, he lunged forward and grabbed Sa'id by the beard. Sa'id, in trying to defend himself, fell backwards on the floor. Umar, seizing the advantage, leapt on his chest, pinned him down and brandished his sword above his head. Fatimah cried out, ran to her husband and grabbing Umar's tunic pulled it with all her strength to drag him from Sa'id's chest.

'Umar! Get off! Let him go!'

Umar, exasperated at the interruption, slapped her hard in the face. A trickle of blood ran down Fatimah's cheek. Hurt and bleeding, she faced Umar bravely.

'O enemy of God', she said, 'you hate us only because we believe in the One God.'

'That's right', said Umar.

'Then do what you like with us, Umar', replied Fatimah, her voice like steel. 'We bear witness that there is no god but the One God and that Muhammad is His Prophet. Nothing you can do will change that, however much you hate it. We shall never abandon Islam.'

The determination and courage in his sister's voice so impressed Umar that it acted like a shower of cold water over his rage. Slowly, the anger drained from his features, he relaxed his hold on Sa'id and drew himself up to his full height.

'Alright, sister', Umar's voice was calmer now, 'then let me see what it is you are reading. If there is any sense in it, you could at least share it with me.'

Fatimah hesitated and looked at her husband.

'I promise not to throw it away. I'll return it to you', Umar assured her.

'Very well', said Fatimah, 'but go and wash first. You are in no condition to touch the words of God.'

As Umar left the room, Khabbab, the instructor, emerged from the other room and scolded them in a loud whisper: 'How can you trust an infidel?... and a man of such violence!'

'I know my brother', answered Fatimah, 'and I have high hopes that Allah will direct him to the right path'.

Khabbab, seeing Umar returning, disappeared again into the back room. With a silent prayer, Fatimah handed the pieces of parchment to her brother.

Umar read:

Whatever is in
The heavens and on earth,
Let it declare
The praises and glory of God:

For He is the Exalted
In might, the Wise.

To Him belongs the kingdom
Of the heavens and the earth:
It is He who gives
Life and death; and He
Has power over all things.

He is the First
And the Last,
The Evident
And the Immanent:
And He has full knowledge
Of all things.

He it is Who created
The heavens and the earth

In six days, and moreover
Firmly sits on the Throne
Of authority. He knows
What enters within the earth
And what comes forth out
Of it, what comes down
From heaven and what mounts
Up to it. And He is
With you wheresoever ye
May be. And God sees
Well all that ye do.

To Him belongs the kingdom
Of the heavens and the earth:
And all affairs are
Referred back to God.

He merges night into day,
And He merges day into night;
And He has full knowledge
Of the secrets of all hearts.*

Previously, Umar would not have understood the words
on the parchment, they would have been as a foreign
language to him; but now he immediately understood
them and they were clearly the truth. A conviction filled
him as he read on,
realising for the first time
that all along he had
been mistaken, and that
Muhammad was indeed
the Messenger from the
One God... for indeed,
how could there be other
gods, besides the One
God?

We have not sent down
The Qur'an to thee to be
An occasion for thy
distress,

But only as an
admonition
To those who fear God,

* al-Hadīd 57: 1–6.

A revelation from Him
Who created the earth
And the heavens on high.

God most Gracious
Firmly sits
On the throne of authority.

To Him belongs what is
In the heavens and on earth,
And all between them,
And all beneath the soil.*

. . .

* Ṭā Hā 20: 2–6.

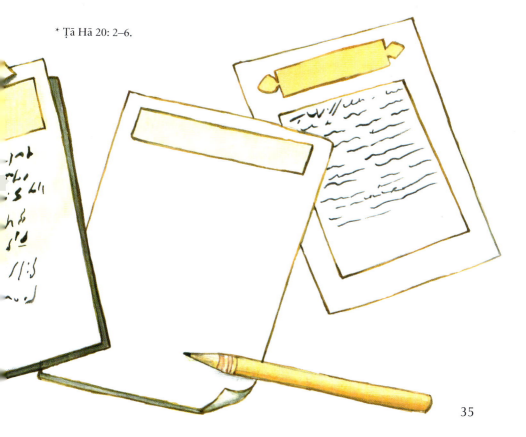

But when he came
To the Fire, a voice
Was heard: O Moses!

Verily, I am thy Lord!
Therefore in My presence
Put off thy shoes: thou art
In the sacred valley Tuwa
I have chosen thee:
Listen, then, to the inspiration
Sent to thee.

Verily, I am God
There is no god but I:
So serve thou Me only,
And establish regular prayer
For celebrating My praise.

Verily the Hour is coming,
My design is to keep it
Hidden, for every soul
To receive its reward
By the measure of
Its Endeavour.

Therefore let not such as
Believe not therein
But follow their own
Lusts, divert thee therefrom,
Lest thou perish!*

'Enough! I need read no more!' declared Umar, with
conviction. 'It is preposterous to associate anyone with the
One God... how could I have ever believed otherwise?...
Quick... where is Muhammad, tell me!'

Sister and brother-in-law stood and looked at Umar,
unsure of his true intentions. Khabbab came out of his
hiding place and whispered to Sa'id: 'Do you think... that
maybe the Prophet's prayer is going to be fulfilled?'

But Sa'id said nothing, then glancing at Fatimah for
approval, he finally told Umar where the Blessed Prophet
Muhammad could be found. Umar sheathed his sword,

---

* Ṭā Hā 20: 11–16.

slung it over his shoulder and started off for Dar Arqam where the Blessed Prophet was staying.

Inside Dar Arqam the Blessed Prophet and his followers were seated reciting a Surah, whilst Hamza and Talha were standing guard at the door. Umar knocked.

'Who is there?' asked Talha.

'Umar', came the response.

The entire assembly looked up in amazement. What could he want, other than to persecute or insult them? Dare they let him in? Hamza, seeing that the Companions were doubtful, spoke up.

'We should not fear him', he said. 'If he has come with good intention, then he will embrace Islam. If not... why look around... there are enough of us to tackle one man, surely!'

Talha, at a sign from Hamza, unbarred the door and opened it. As soon as Umar stepped inside Hamza and Talha seized his arms and took him to where the Blessed Prophet was sitting.

The Blessed Prophet looked up. 'Let him go', he told them, and moved calmly towards Umar. Umar made not a move. The Blessed Prophet reached up to Umar's neck, took hold of his sword strap and pulled the sword towards him. Umar, strong and ferocious Umar, stood before his enemy but was incapable of making a move. He began to tremble and shake from his head to his feet. The Blessed Prophet looked into his eyes.

'Umar', he said, 'give up your wrong ways before God's curse falls upon you. Umar, accept Islam. O Allah, guide his heart to the right path.'

'Wha... what should I say?' stammered Umar.

Hamza spoke up. 'Say that you bear witness that there is but One God and that Muhammad is His Messenger.'

Umar looked at Hamza, then at the Blessed Prophet. 'I bear witness...' he began; the followers were all watching him with baited breath. Umar had stopped shaking and now drew himself up to his full height. 'I bear witness that there is but One God and that you, Muhammad, are His true Messenger.'

At the declaration of the *Kalimah* spoken by Umar, the Muslims could contain themselves no longer. They all cried as in one voice, *'Allahu Akbar!* God is the Most Great!' The shouting was so loud, and so full of joy, they say, that it resounded throughout the streets of Makka. Umar, caught up in the enthusiasm of his newly found faith and the reaction of the Believers, shouted with them the very words which he had so often scowled at a short time ago: *'Allahu Akbar! Allahu Akbar!'*

From that moment on, Umar brought the Muslims the strength, courage and leadership abilities which he had once used against them.

Immediately, he became as enthusiastic and loud in his support of Islam as he had been before in opposing it.

'Tell me, O Messenger of God', he asked, 'are we not in the path of the truth whether we live or die?'

'Yes, surely', replied the Blessed Prophet. 'It is time now for us to go out openly and claim our right to pray in the Ka'ba.'

'Well then', said Umar, turning to the others with outstretched arms, 'let us go and pray in front of whomever we will! Now that Umar is with you, there is no need to hide from anyone!'

The Blessed Prophet nodded, smiled and gave his consent.

Out of Arqam's house they marched, in two rows, one led by Umar and the other by Hamza, Makka's two fearless leaders. Down the street they filed, to the surprise of citizens along the way, into the Haram they went, and before the eyes of their astounded opponents, began their Islamic Prayer.

Now that Umar had become a Muslim he was also ashamed, deep down, of the persecution he had inflicted on his fellow Believers. He was eager to right the matter by putting himself in the same position. The first person to whom he thought of declaring his new belief was the greatest enemy of Islam: the Blessed Prophet's uncle and

respected leader of the Quraysh, Abu Jahl himself.

So, the very next day after his declaration, Umar went straight to Abu Jahl's house. With head held high and shoulders squared, he knocked loudly.

'Who is there?'asked Abu Jahl.

'Son of Khattab', replied Umar, and Abu Jahl opened the door.

Umar looked down on the venerated leader of the Quraysh. 'I have come to announce', he declared, 'that I have given up the religion of my forefathers'.

Umar awaited the expected attack, in either words or action, but none came. Abu Jahl was stunned. The man is drunk, he thought to himself, or he has had too much sun. I'd better humour him rather than turn that giant's wrath upon me...

'Really?' he croaked.

'Yes, really!' roared Umar, expecting a fight.

But Abu Jahl just stood a moment, then said in a low voice:'Don't do that, Umar.'

Umar became frustrated. 'I shall never give up Islam, never!'

Abu Jahl, shocked, angry and afraid, hurriedly retreated inside his house and slammed the door in Umar's face.

Umar could not believe it. Nothing had come of his announcement! Turning on his heel, he marched down the street and knocked on the door of two more tribal chiefs. One, deciding that Umar must be drunk, refused to argue with him, and the other quickly changed the subject of conversation. Umar shook his head in bewilderment. What was wrong with these people that they didn't want to challenge him? He tried declaring his belief to a third man who was walking in his direction. Realising that Umar was serious, the man told him:

'Look, Umar. If you really want everyone to know that you have embraced Islam, then you should go and tell Jamil, son of Muammir... the greatest gossip in town. Once he hears about it, the news will spread like wildfire.'

Umar thought this was an excellent idea; so at dusk, when everyone had assembled in the Haram, Umar went up to Jamil and told him of his conversion to Islam. Jamil couldn't wait. Bursting with this astounding piece of news, he cried aloud to all present:

'Lo! Citizens of Makka!, the son of Khattab has become a heretic!'

But Umar would have none of that. 'Idiot', he said, pushing him aside. 'This man's a liar!' he shouted.

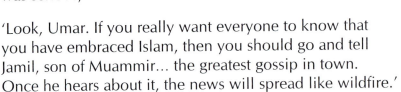

44

'Now hear the truth! I, Umar, son of Khattab, have
declared for all the world to hear: There is no god but the
One God and Muhammad is His Messenger.'

The assembly was appalled. What was happening here,
the enemy of Muhammad had become a turncoat and
was now on his side? So shocked were the braver ones by
this announcement, they forgot about Umar's powerful
build and rushed at him, beating him with their fists and
threatening him with their swords.

This was exactly what Umar wanted. One by one, he
fought them off: a blow here, a sword-slash there. 'This
follower of Muhammad is no weakling!' he cried.' Taste
the sword of Allah.' Umar received quite a few blows in
the skirmish, but in the end, the attackers all fell back to
nurse their wounds, and Umar stood alone in the empty
Haram, having tasted the pain of chastisement as well as
the fruits of victory.